PO

A Lion
to Guard Us

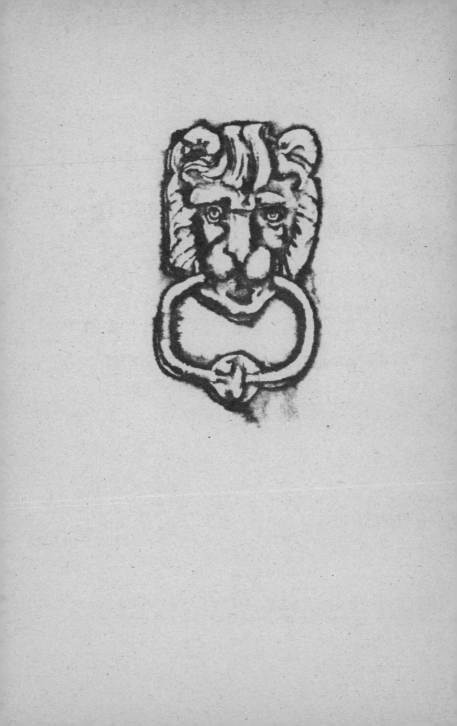

A Lion to Guard Us

by CLYDE ROBERT BULLA

illustrated by MICHELE CHESSARE

SCHOLASTIC BOOK SERVICES
NEW YORK • TORONTO • LONDON • AUCKLAND • SYDNEY • TOKYO

To Marilyn Kriney

ISBN 0-590-32878-6

Text copyright © 1981 by Clyde Robert Bulla. Illustrations copyright © 1981 by Michele Chessare. All rights reserved. A Thomas Y. Crowell Book published by Scholastic Book Services, a division of Scholastic Inc., 730 Broadway, New York, NY 10003, by arrangement with Harper & Row, Publishers, Inc.

12 11 10 9 8 7 6 5 4 3 2 1   3   3 4 5 6/8
Printed in the U.S.A.   11

Contents

I   The Sailor Man   1

II   A Story   7

III   Dr. Crider   14

IV   Time and Work   20

V   The House on Philpot Lane   25

VI   Out the Door   30

VII   Night People   35

VIII   A Piece of Luck   41

IX   A Great World   45

X   The Sea Adventure   49

XI   The Hold   55

XII   Near the Sea   59

XIII   The Devil Doll   65

XIV   Brass or Gold?   68

XV   The Storm   72

XVI   Ashore   79

XVII   The Island   82

XVIII   The Smallest House   87

XIX   A Fire at Night   92

XX   A Quarrel   96

XXI   Waiting for Jemmy   100

XXII   The Other Side of the Island   105

XXIII   The Lion's Head   110

I

The Sailor Man

On a February morning in the year 1609, a small,
thin-faced man made his way over London Bridge.
He wore a leather jacket and a blue wool stocking
cap. His clothes were splashed with mud, and mud
sucked at his shoes. He could hardly see for the
cold rain in his face.

He had been looking for Fish Street, and here
it was, at the end of London Bridge. Now he was
looking for a house on Fish Street—a great stone
house not far from the bridge.

Here was one with tall chimneys and many windows. It must be the house, he thought. He went
around to the back.

A plump, pretty maid opened the door.

"Would this be the Trippett house?" he asked.

She looked at his muddy clothes. "What do you want?"

"A word with Mistress Freebold, if she's about."

"Mistress Freebold? Oh, you mean Annie. You can't see her," said the maid. "She's sick abed."

"Could you just let her know there's someone here from America—?"

"America?" The maid stared into his face. "Then you must be—" She was gone. He heard her crying out, "Amanda, Amanda!"

Someone came running. Someone cried, "Father!" and a girl was there. She looked no more than ten or eleven—a pale little thing with great, dark eyes.

She stopped. She said in bitter disappointment, "You're not my father."

"I shouldn't think so," said the man.

"Ellie said you were from America, and she thought—I thought—"

"So you're James Freebold's girl," he said.

"One of them. I'm Amanda." She asked quickly, "Do you know my father?"

"I do, and I saw him not many weeks ago. We were together in America, in the colony of Virginia. I'm a sailor, you see, and my ship was there—"

"And you saw him." Her eyes were bright again. "Was he well? What did he say?"

"He was well enough, for all I could see. He'd built a house in Jamestown. That's the only town there. When my ship sailed, he asked if I'd stop for a word with his family in London. He thinks of you each day. He prays you will all be together before another year is out."

Tears came to her eyes. "When you see him, will you tell him—?"

"I'll not be seeing him again," the man broke in. "It's a long, hard voyage to Virginia. I'll not be going back."

"Oh," she said.

Someone was calling, "Amanda!"

"You're wanted," he said. "I'll take my leave."

"But you'll come again?"

He shook his head. "I've told my tale. Good-day to you."

He left her. He was gone, and she didn't know his name or where to find him again, and there were

a hundred things she hadn't asked. She hadn't even said thank you.

She took a step after him, but Cook's voice called her back. "A-*man*-da!"

She closed the door. She went down the long, cold hall and into the kitchen.

Cook was at the table, beating eggs. Her face was red. Her cap was over one eye.

"Who gave you leave to stand in the door and talk all day?" she said. "Who was that man?"

Ellie the maid came out of the pantry. "Oh, Amanda, was it your father?"

The door to the back stairs opened. A small boy put his head out. "Was it Father?" he asked.

"Jemmy!" cried Amanda. "You know you're not to come in here. No, it wasn't Father."

His head disappeared, and the door closed.

Amanda told Cook and Ellie, "It was a sailor man back from Virginia. He saw my father there. He *talked* to him. Father is well—and he's built a house—and he thinks of us—"

Cook gave a snort. "He does, does he? He thinks of you so much that he sails off and leaves you for three whole years."

"Oh, that's cruel!" said Ellie.

"Hold your tongue, miss," said Cook, "and Amanda, you get back to your work."

She went off into the pantry.

As soon as Cook was gone, Amanda opened the door to the back stairs. The small boy was sitting on the steps. A smaller girl sat beside him.

"It wasn't Father. It was a sailor man," Amanda said. "But he *saw* Father. Just think of that. I'll tell you about it tonight."

"Will it be a story?" asked the boy.

"It will be *like* a story," said Amanda, and she shut the door.

II

A Story

Mistress Trippett and all her family had had their supper. The servants had been fed. Amanda was in the kitchen alone.

She had just washed the pots and pans and hung them over the fireplace to dry. She looked in at her brother and sister on the back stairs. They were asleep. Jemmy's head was against the wall. Meg's head was against his shoulder.

It hurt her to see them there, like two puppies that nobody wanted. Why couldn't they come into the kitchen and be warm?

But Cook wouldn't have it.

"They'd be under our feet," she said. "They've got their own room. Let them stay in it."

Amanda had stood up to her. "They're not to be shut away in a room all day. It's bad enough to leave them on the stairs. But at least they're next to the kitchen where they won't be so lonely."

She looked at them sleeping there. Jemmy was getting to be a big boy. He would be a fine, strong man like his father. But Meg was too small, too thin.

Amanda woke them. She gave them their supper—beef stew with bread and butter.

"Eat," she said, "while I go to Mother."

Mother was in a room down the hall. Once all four of them had lived in the room. It had been almost like a home.

Now it was a sickroom. The little ones could not stay there. Mistress Trippett had put them into a tiny room in the back of the house, and they slept there at night.

Sometimes Amanda slept with them. Sometimes she sat up all night—half-asleep, half-awake—by her mother's bed.

She carried a lighted candle to the sickroom.

Mother lay with her eyes closed. She had not left her bed since the day before Christmas. That was the day she had fallen on the stairs.

But she had been ill long before that.

Amanda sat by the bed and took her mother's hand. She began to tell her about the man who had come from America, but she soon stopped.

"Why do you talk to her?" Cook had said. "It's like talking to the wall. She doesn't even know you're there."

And it did seem to be true.

Ellie looked in. "Do you want me to sit for a while?"

"Oh, *would* you, Ellie? I want to put the little ones to bed and talk to them a bit."

Amanda went back to Jemmy and Meg. They had eaten their supper. She took them to their room.

They had a pallet for a bed. Mistress Trippett had given them some covers. One was a piece of red velvet curtain, faded and old. Jemmy liked to wear it for a cloak and play the fine gentleman.

Amanda put the candle on the floor. She sat in the middle of the pallet. Jemmy and Meg lay down on either side. She tucked the covers about them to keep out the cold.

"Now," she said, "I'll tell you a story."

"About Father and the lion?" asked Jemmy.

"I've told you that," she said. "I've told you and told you."

"No, you haven't," he said. "Not for a long time."

So Amanda began, "Once a man came to London to seek his fortune."

"That's Father," said Jemmy.

"Yes," she said.

"His name was James Freebold," said Jemmy. "That's my name, too. That's my real name."

"He met a beautiful maiden with golden hair—"

"That's Mother," said Jemmy.

"—and they were married and had three children."

"Three *fine* children," said Jemmy.

"James Freebold was a carpenter. He could build houses. Do you remember the house we used to have? He built it for us—"

"I know," said Jemmy. "Tell the story."

"There is a land called America," said Amanda. "Some call it the New World. It's across the sea, and it's a beautiful land with rivers and trees and birds. Indians live there, and they wear feathers and shoot with bows and arrows. Some men asked Father to go there with them to help build houses. They were going to build houses and towns and live in America in a place called—"

"Virginia," said Meg.

"Yes. You like that name, don't you, Meggie? Father said even if we were poor in London, we would be rich in Virginia. We would have our own fields and gardens. Remember the song he used to sing?" She sang very softly:

There are lands a-calling me
From across the wide, blue sea,
And I'll find a home one day
In a fair land far away.

"Tell the *story*," said Jemmy.

"Well, you and Meg and I had to wait with Mother. Virginia was a wild place. It wasn't ready for women and children. Father went ahead, and we moved to Mistress Trippett's, because Mother worked there."

"You didn't tell it all," said Jemmy.

"Yes, I did."

"No. You left out the lion."

"Oh," said Amanda. "There was a door knocker

on the house where we used to live. Before Father went away, he took it off and gave it to us."

"He gave it to me," said Jemmy.

"He gave it to us all. It was a lion's head. He said it was a lion to guard us while he was gone."

Jemmy said again, "He gave it to me." From under the covers he took out a small lion's head made of brass. A brass bar hung from its mouth. He swung the bar back and forth.

"Don't you want to hear about the sailor man?" asked Amanda. "He was here today. He'd been to Virginia, and he saw Father there. Father has a house, and he wants us to come."

"When?"

"We have to wait."

"Why?"

"For Mother to get well. Now go to sleep. You, too, Meg."

She waited until they were asleep before she slipped out of bed. She picked up the candle and went back to Mother's room.

III

Dr. Crider

Ellie said the next morning, "It's been awhile since Mistress came downstairs. This might be the day."

At least once a week Mistress Trippett surprised them in the kitchen to make sure that all was neat and no one was idle.

And just after breakfast, they heard the click of her heels on the front stairs.

"I told you!" whispered Ellie.

The servants stood like soldiers. Mistress Trippett came down into the kitchen. She looked small, even in her high heels and her tall, red wig. Her eyes were like little black beads.

She swept through the kitchen. She peered into the pantry and the cupboards. She opened the door to the back stairs.

Amanda held her breath. Jemmy and Meg were there. Once Mistress Trippett had called them idle brats. But today she almost smiled as she shut the door.

"The children have grown," she said. "How old is the boy?"

"Eight, ma'am," answered Amanda.

"And the girl?"

"Only five, ma'am." Suddenly Amanda felt bold. "Do you think they might come into the kitchen?"

"Why, certainly," said Mistress Trippett, and she swept off upstairs.

Cook's face was like stone. "I'll not have those brats under my feet."

"You will if Mistress says so," said Ellie.

Cook struck at her with a spoon. Ellie jumped out of the way.

Cook suddenly shouted at Amanda, "Don't stand there like a noddy. Fetch some water!"

Amanda took up the water pail and ran.

The pump was on the street, two doors down.

She pumped the pail full. It was a heavy, wooden pail. Filled with water, it was as much as she could lift. Every few steps she had to put it down.

Someone came up beside her. "Amanda!" said a voice.

A man was there. He was dressed in black. His beard was gray, and there were little lines about his mouth that gave him a friendly look.

"Good-day, Dr. Crider," she said.

"Child, you can't carry that." He tried to take the pail, but she held on to it with both hands.

"Thank you, sir, but they wouldn't like it if you carried the water."

"Who wouldn't?"

"Cook and Mistress Trippett."

"They needn't know."

"Mistress looks out the window. She might be looking now. Besides, it's *my* work."

"Why?"

"I'm taking Mother's place." Amanda carried the pail a few steps and set it down again. "Are you here to see Mother?"

"Yes," he said. "How is she?"

"Better, I think. Today she looked brighter."

"Amanda, don't you have a father?"

"Oh, yes," she answered. "He's in America."

"America! I never knew that," he said in surprise. "Did he go to the colony in Virginia?"

"Yes, sir. He's in Jamestown."

"America. The New World," said Dr. Crider. "That's an old dream of mine. If I were a young man, I'd be there today."

"We are all going there—my mother and brother and sister and I," she told him. "We're going as soon as Mother is well."

"Are you, indeed?" he said. They had come to the house, and they parted there. He went to the front door, she to the back.

It was more than a week before she saw him again.

Late one afternoon she thought she heard his voice in the hall. She asked Ellie, "Is the doctor here?"

Ellie looked at Cook. They both looked at her, and neither spoke.

"I want to see him," said Amanda. "May I go?"

"Finish your work," said Cook.

The kitchen began to grow dark. Amanda was lighting candles when Dr. Crider came into the room. He looked tired. The lines in his face were deeper.

"Amanda—" he said.

"Yes, sir?"

"Will you come with me?"

She went with him into the hall. They were alone there.

"I must tell you something," he said.

She looked into his face.

"Amanda, your mother is dead."

She stood still.

"I'm sorry," he said. "I did what I could."

She felt as if she were choking. She put her hands to her mouth.

"Did you hear me, child?"

She nodded.

"Do you want me to tell your brother and sister?"

She tried to speak.

He asked again, "Did you hear me?"

"Yes," she whispered.

"And shall I tell your brother and sister?"

She spoke then. "No, sir. It's for me to tell them."

IV

Time and Work

Mistress Trippett said, "It's a sad thing, but time and work will help you forget. Time and work, Amanda."

"Yes, ma'am," said Amanda.

She did her work. That helped her through the days. But at night she lay awake. She tried to think, and she asked herself, What's to be done? What's to be done now?

One day she went out back to feed the chickens. Jemmy and Meg were at work in the garden, clearing off the dry weeds and sticks. Jemmy had been raking. He had left the rake in the path, and Amanda tripped over it.

"Why don't you watch where you leave things!"
she shouted. She caught hold of Jemmy and shook
him.

His mouth fell open. He looked hurt and surprised.

She ran back into the house. She was almost crying
as she bumped into Ellie in the hall.

"I shook Jemmy," she said. "What ever made
me do it? I'm the one to look after him and Meg,
and I—"

"You *do* look after them," said Ellie.

"No! I don't mend their clothes. I never talk to
them anymore—"

Ellie said, "Don't be putting blame on yourself.
Life is hard for you now. When you lose someone
it's like—like having to find your way again."

Amanda grew quiet. It was true, what Ellie had
said.

That night, in bed with Jemmy and Meg, she left
the candle burning. She said, "Who wants a story?"

"You said you didn't know any," said Jemmy.

"I didn't, but now I do."

"Is it about Father?" he asked.

"It's more about two sisters and their brother."

"That's you and Meggie and I," he said.

"And one of the sisters was a crosspatch," said Amanda.

"That's you," said Jemmy.

"She'd lost her way," said Amanda.

"What?"

"She'd lost her way, but she found it again, so she wasn't a crosspatch anymore."

"Is that all the story?" he asked.

"No. The brother and sisters lived in the city of London in the country of England. And one day— do you know what they did?"

"What?" he said.

"They went away. They left the city of London and the country of England. They left it all behind them."

He sat up. "Where did they go?"

"They got on a big ship, and they sailed to America. They saw a town. That was Jamestown. They saw a man, and he came to meet them."

"Father!" said Jemmy.

"Father," said Meg.

"When are we going?" asked Jemmy.

"I don't know yet," said Amanda, "but we *are* going. We *are!*"

In the morning she asked Cook, "If it please you, may I go outside?"

"No," said Cook. "Where?"

"To the next street over."

"What's on the next street over?"

"It's where the Virginia Company is."

"The Virginia Company? What may that be?"

"It's the company that sends out ships to America."

"And what's that to you?"

"Jemmy and Meg and I—we're going," said Amanda.

Cook gave a snort. "And I'm going to fly to the moon!"

"If it please you," said Amanda, "the house is on Philpot Lane. That's only a step away. I'll be back in no time at all."

"No, you won't," said Cook, "because you're not going."

All morning Amanda worked. She swept and scrubbed. She mixed the bread and peeled the onions.

Toward noon, Cook shouted in her ear, "You've let the water pail go empty again!"

Amanda took up the pail and ran with it. Outside the back door she looked behind her. No one was watching.

She set the pail behind a currant bush. She picked up her skirts and went flying down the alley.

V

The House on Philpot Lane

Amanda went straight to the big brick house on Philpot Lane. No one answered her knock. She tried the door, and it opened. She went into a large room where men sat at tables. They were writing, and she could hear the scratch of pens on paper.

She chose the man with the kindest face. "If it please you," she said, "can you tell me about the ships that sail to Virginia?"

He kept on writing. It looked as if he were setting down figures and adding them up.

"I was here once with my mother," she told him. "We wanted to go to Virginia because my father is there. A man said to come back later."

She thought he hadn't heard. She made ready to say it all again. But he had stopped writing.

"Your father's name?" he asked.

"James Freebold."

He opened a book and ran his finger down the pages. "Yes, he's here."

"We want to go on the next ship," she said.

"There will be ships going next month," he said. "How many are you?"

"Three."

"Your names?"

"Jemmy and Meg, and I'm Amanda."

"Is Meg your mother?"

"No, sir. My mother is dead. Meg is my sister."

"How old is your sister?"

"Five."

"How old is Jemmy?"

"Eight."

"But—you're only children. You can't go to the New World with no one to look after you."

"I can look after us."

"No, that won't do. We might find someone to look after you on the voyage, but that would take money—"

"I have money," she said.

"How much?"

"I don't know, but—"

"See here, little girl, this is a busy place, and I'm a busy man." He dipped his pen into the ink and went back to writing.

"Please—" she began, but he didn't speak to her or look at her again.

She went home. The pail was still behind the currant bush. She took it to the pump and filled it.

When she carried it into the kitchen, Cook asked, "What kept you?"

Amanda set down the pail of water.

"You went to that place, didn't you?" asked Cook. "*Didn't* you?"

"Yes," said Amanda.

"Wait till I tell Mistress Trippett."

"I'm going to tell her myself." Amanda started upstairs.

Cook gave a scream. "You can't go up the front stairs!"

Amanda went on. She knocked at the door of Mistress Trippett's sitting room.

"Who is it?" came Mistress Trippett's voice.

"If it please you, ma'am—"

Mistress Trippett opened the door. Her wig was off. She looked angry. "What are *you* doing up here?"

"I wanted to tell you—I went to the house where the Virginia Company is."

"Well?"

"There are ships going to the New World next month."

"Well?"

"Jemmy and Meg and I—we're going."

Mistress Trippett's mouth was thin. "I thought you'd put that nonsense out of your head."

"Oh, no, ma'am. We have to go where Father is."

"Your father doesn't want you. He forgot about you long ago."

"No—" began Amanda.

"Even if he did want you, you'd be a fool to go. Virginia is a terrible place, full of wild Indians and wild beasts. All those tales about the New World and how wonderful it is—they're lies, all lies!"

"But we have to go—"

"You have to do nothing of the kind. I've fed you and put clothes on your back. I've given you the best home you've ever had. Would you give up all this? Would you go starve in a strange land where you'd never come out alive?"

"Father—"

"What has your father done for you? Ask yourself that. Then ask yourself what *I've* done for you!" And Mistress Trippett slammed the door.

VI

Out the Door

That evening Amanda and Ellie met in the pantry.
"I heard Mistress Trippett," said Ellie. "She doesn't
want you to go."

"But she knew we were going to the New
World," said Amanda. "Mother told her that when
we came here."

"She thought you'd forget about it," said Ellie.
"She wants to keep you here. You work hard, and
you don't eat much. And Jemmy and Meg are coming on. She'll put them to work, too, and you'll
all be working free."

"Oh!" said Amanda. "I forgot to ask about the
money."

"Money?"

"When Father went away, he sold our house. He gave the money to Mother, and she kept it in a purse. Mistress Trippett has it."

"How do you know?"

"Mother had it on a string around her neck. That day she fell downstairs, Cook and I put her to bed. Mistress Trippett came in, and she took the purse. She said she was keeping it for us."

"You'd best forget about it."

"It's ours, and we need it," said Amanda. "Jemmy and Meg and I—we need it to go on the ship."

"Well, you'd best take care how you ask her," said Ellie. "She's already upset. You'd best wait a long time."

"We can't wait long. The ship sails next month."

But Amanda waited a week. Then she went back upstairs.

This time Mistress Trippett let her into the sitting room. Her oldest son, Randolph, was there. He was a roly-poly man with pale, fishy eyes.

He didn't look at Amanda. "I'll get my coat, Mother, and meet you downstairs," he said, and he went out.

Mistress Trippett was dressed for a party, in

cherry-colored silk. She smiled at herself in the mirror.

"I know why you're here," she said to Amanda. "You came to say you're sorry. You came to say you're going to be a good girl. And if you *are* a good girl, I'll forget the foolish things you said."

"Please, ma'am—"

"Well?" said Mistress Trippett. "I haven't much time."

"Please, ma'am," said Amanda, "will you give me the money?"

Mistress Trippett turned from the mirror. "*What?*"

"The money you kept for us."

"What's that you're saying? The *money*—?"

"It was in the little purse—around Mother's neck."

Mistress Trippett's face had gone white. "And who do you think paid the doctor? Who do you think gave you everything you have? Who do you think kept a roof over your head?"

"But I worked, ma'am," said Amanda, "and Mother, too, as long as she could."

"And now you say I stole your money!"

"I *never* said that!" cried Amanda.

But Mistress Trippett was past hearing. She picked up a book and threw it. It barely missed Amanda's head.

Randolph came running.

Mistress Trippett pointed at Amanda. "Get her out of here! Get her out, before I—"

Randolph seized Amanda and pushed her out of the room.

She ran down into the kitchen.

"What have you done?" asked Cook.

"What did you say to her?" asked Ellie.

"I only asked for the money," said Amanda.

Jemmy and Meg crept out from under the table.

"Amanda—" said Jemmy, and he sounded scared.

Randolph came down the stairs. He said to Cook, "Mother's fainted away. Go help her." He said to Ellie, "Run for the doctor." He saw Amanda. "You little pig, you're the cause of it all. Get out of this house, and take those brats with you. Get out, and don't ever show your face here again!"

He reached for her. He tripped over Jemmy and fell to his knees.

Amanda heard Ellie say, "Oh, run!"

She caught hold of Jemmy and Meg, and they ran, out the back door and into the night.

VII

Night People

They went toward the lights of London Bridge. Amanda could feel her heart thumping. She had a pain in her side from running so fast.

"Are we going over the bridge?" asked Jemmy.

"No," said Amanda.

There was trouble on the bridge. Two wagons had run into each other. One had lost a wheel. The drivers had gotten out and begun to fight.

Amanda led Jemmy and Meg away from the bridge. They saw an inn ahead. Lights shone from the windows. Jemmy pulled Amanda toward it. She pulled back. "We can't go there."

"Why?"

"It's only for those with money."

They walked along the river. On the riverbank, people were sitting about small fires.

"Who are they?" asked Jemmy.

"People with no homes," answered Amanda.

"Like us," said Jemmy.

Some of the people were cooking. The smell of food was in the air.

"I'm hungry," said Jemmy.

"You had your supper," said Amanda.

"I'm glad I'm not *very* hungry," he said.

They came to an old wooden pier. They walked out on it and sat down. The darkness hid them. They could hear the soft splash of the river below.

"Will they come after us?" asked Jemmy.

"No, unless—" A thought had come to Amanda. "Unless Mistress Trippett dies. Then they'll say I'm to blame, and they'll come after me."

"What will they do if they find you?"

"Put me in jail."

"Would Meg and I go, too?"

"No."

"Where would we go?"

"Jemmy, hush."

"Where would we go, Amanda?"

"You'd go to a place where you work all day and half the night. When you're poor and don't have anywhere else to go, that's what you do."

"Meg's too little."

"So are you."

"No, I'm not. But I don't want to go there. I'd rather go to jail with you."

"We won't be going to jail," she said, "because they won't catch us."

"Where *are* we going?"

"I don't know yet, but we're going to stay together. Do you hear that, Jemmy? Do you hear, Meg?"

"I hear," he said.

Meg said nothing. She'd said nothing since they had left Mistress Trippett's.

Meg was too quiet, too *good.* All her life she'd been pushed away into corners. *Sit there, Meg. Don't move, Meg.* She'd never played like other children. She didn't know how.

A woman was coming slowly toward them with a lantern in her hand. She stopped at the pier, and the light shone on her face. She was very old. Her eyes looked hollow and wild.

"Give me—give me," she said.

"We've nothing to give," said Amanda.

The old woman held the lantern high. She was looking at Meg.

"It's my little girl," she said.

"No," said Amanda.

The old woman came closer. "Don't you know me, dear?"

"Go away," said Amanda.

The old woman sat down beside them. She touched Meg's hair. "Come, dear, I'll take you home with me."

"Leave her alone!" Amanda pulled Meg away and took Jemmy's hand.

They left the pier. The old woman called after them, "Wait—wait!" but they didn't stop.

They walked back toward London Bridge. Now Amanda could see that the night people were everywhere. They were in alleys and doorways. They were part of the shadows.

The spring night was not cold, but Amanda was shivering. Where could they go to be away from

these people? Where could they go to be alone, to rest and sleep a little?

They came to Fish Street.

She said, "If we go back to Mistress Trippett's—"

"We can't go back," said Jemmy. "You know what Fat Randolph said."

"We wouldn't go in. If we went into the garden . . . No one goes there after dark. We could hide behind the chicken coops. In the morning, before it gets light, we could be gone."

They walked up the street. Mistress Trippett's house was in sight, with lights in the windows.

There was a man in the alley beside the house. He carried a lantern. He came toward them.

He would go by, Amanda thought. But no. He was stopping.

She could only stand there, with Jemmy holding one of her hands and Meg the other.

"Amanda—?" asked the man.

She knew him then. It was Dr. Crider.

VIII

A Piece of Luck

"I've been up and down the street looking for you," said the doctor. "It was a piece of luck I found you. Were you coming back to Mistress Trippett's?"

"No, sir—not to the house," answered Amanda. "Master Randolph put us out."

"So I heard," said Dr. Crider. "And where did Master Randolph think you might go, after dark in the middle of London?"

"We didn't know where to go," said Amanda. "I thought we might find a place behind the house."

"You'd better come with me," he said.

They walked together. The lantern bobbed along, lighting their way.

"If it please you—" began Amanda.

"Yes?"

"Did you see Mistress Trippett tonight?"

"I did. A girl came to fetch me. She said Mistress Trippett was in a faint."

"And she didn't die?"

"Die? Of course not. It was only a fit of temper."

They turned off Fish Street. They walked along a row of wooden houses. Dr. Crider stopped at one of them.

"Where are we?" asked Jemmy.

"I've brought you home with me," said Dr. Crider.

They went inside. A night lamp burned in the hallway.

The house was not poor, but neither was it fine. The rooms were small. The walls were bare.

"Have you had supper?" asked Dr. Crider.

"Yes, sir," answered Amanda.

"Then perhaps you'll sit with me while I have mine." He led them into the kitchen.

They all sat at the table while he drank a mug of milk and ate a cold meat pie. Amanda looked about the kitchen. With Dr. Crider's leave, she thought, she would sweep up the crumbs. She would polish the copper pots and pans until they shone.

"They said you made Mistress Trippett fall in a faint," said the doctor. "Poor Mistress Trippett, what did you do to her?"

"I only asked for the money."

"What money?"

"Father left it when he went away. Mistress Trippett was keeping it. I don't see why I was wrong to ask for it."

"You weren't wrong," he said.

"But we'll never get it now, and we need it—to go to America. Ships will be going soon."

"How soon?"

"Next month."

He had finished his supper.

"Shall I clear the things away?" she asked.

"No. Sit awhile." He asked, "Is your father happy in the New World?"

"I don't know, sir."

"Doesn't he write to you?"

"He never learned writing or reading," she answered. "None of us ever learned. There may be a school in Jamestown one day, and then—"

"Jamestown," he said. "That's where your father is?"

"Yes, sir." She looked at Jemmy and Meg. They had gone to sleep, with their heads on the table. She was so tired she wanted to lay her head beside theirs.

Dr. Crider pushed back his chair. "Time for bed," he said.

He gave them a room of their own. It had a bed, not just a pallet on the floor.

"Lie down," he said. "There—I'll tuck you in."

That was the last thing Amanda remembered before she went to sleep.

IX

A Great World

It was morning when she woke. Dr. Crider was in the doorway, dressed to go out.

"I'll be back soon," he said. "Do you know how to make breakfast? Of course, you do. Have whatever you can find in the kitchen. I've already eaten."

He was gone.

Jemmy and Meg were still asleep. She went out into the kitchen. A small fire burned in the grate. She swung the kettle over it. Almost at once it began to sing. She set out a plate of biscuits. She made tea in a round blue pot.

Jemmy and Meg came to the door. Their hair

was on end. Their eyes were sleepy.

"Where is this place?" asked Jemmy.

"Don't you remember?" said Amanda. "Dr. Crider brought us here. Come and have your tea. See? Here's a biscuit to dip in it. There's one for you, too, Meg."

They came to the table. Something clanked as Jemmy sat down.

"What was that?" asked Amanda.

"The knock-knock," said Meg.

Jemmy put his hand into his pocket and took out the little brass door knocker.

"Jemmy!" said Amanda. "You had it all the time."

"I keep it in my pocket," he said. "Aren't you glad? Now Mistress Trippett and Fat Randolph won't get it."

"You can't carry it that way," said Amanda. "You'll wear out your pocket."

"How *shall* I carry it?"

"I don't know. We'll think of a way. Put it on the table for now."

He put the lion's head down beside his cup. Amanda thought of what Father had said. "A lion to guard you . . ."

After breakfast she set to work. Jemmy and Meg

helped her, and they cleaned the kitchen.

Amanda said, "Dr. Crider will be surprised."

But when he came in, he hardly looked at the kitchen. For a while he hardly looked at them. He sat down with his hat and cloak on. His eyes were bright, and there was color in his cheeks.

Amanda spoke to him twice before he answered.

"Yes? What is it?"

"Will you have tea?" she asked.

"Tea? No, no," he said. "Amanda—?"

"Yes, sir?"

"Am I an old man?"

"Yes, sir," she answered.

"I am?"

"I mean—not a *very* old man, but—"

"I know how I must look to you, but don't believe what you see. Today I'm young again. I'm young, Amanda! . . . You don't understand me, do you?"

"No, sir."

"I've just been to see Sir Thomas Smythe on Philpot Lane. We've talked about ships to the New World. Nine are leaving next month. Nine ships, Amanda, leaving in June. And you'll be on one of them."

"I will? Truly?"

"Yes. And Jemmy and Meg, too."

She said, "I know. You went to Mistress Trippett's. You got the money."

"No. Poor Mistress Trippett," he said, "shut up in her big house. Poor Mistress Trippett with her bags of money—let her keep it all. There's a great world outside, and she'll never know it. But *we'll* know it, Amanda."

He was on his feet, walking up and down. "They want me in Jamestown. They *need* me there. They want doctors, and they don't care how old I am. There's nothing to keep me here, and I'm going. We're all going to the New World together!"

X

The Sea Adventure

The time was short, and there was much to do. Dr. Crider had to sell his house. There were things they needed to buy. He made a list.

"We need sea chests," he said. "One for my medicines, two for our clothes."

"Jemmy and Meg and I—we won't need a chest," said Amanda. "We've no clothes besides what we're wearing."

"This will change," said Dr. Crider.

He took them to a street of shops. There they bought dresses and petticoats, breeches and shirts, shoes and stockings.

"If I had cloth, I could sew for us all," said Amanda.

So they looked at cloth and bought some. She turned away from the stripes and flowers that were so beautiful. She chose plain browns and greens.

And one day, in the dark of the morning, they were on their way. A coach took them along the river to where a boat was waiting. They went aboard.

It was an old tub of a boat, small and crowded with people.

"Are we going to America on *this?*" asked Jemmy.

"No, child," said Dr. Crider. "This is only a packet."

A packet, he told them, was a boat that carried people and mail along the coast. "This will take us to the southwest of England. That is where Plymouth is, and Plymouth is where the ships are."

The packet was slow. It was the evening of the fifth day before they came to the town of Plymouth. Ships, large and small, filled the harbor.

"One of them is ours," said Dr. Crider.

They stayed at an inn that night. When Amanda

woke the next morning, Meg was sleeping beside her. Jemmy was up and leaning out the window. Dr. Crider was gone.

"Come and look," said Jemmy. "You never saw so many ships. And little boats are going out to them and coming back again. I think they're loading things on the ships. Come and see, Amanda. Meg, come and see!"

All three were at the window when Dr. Crider came in.

"News, wonderful news!" he said. "Our ship is the *Sea Adventure.* We're sailing with the admiral!"

They were quiet, looking at him.

"You don't know what that means, do you?" he asked.

"No, sir," said Amanda.

"I'll tell you what it means. There are nine ships sailing to Virginia. Each one has a captain. Do you know what a captain is?"

"The captain is the master," said Jemmy.

"Of course, he is. He is master of his ship. But on our voyage, one man is admiral. The admiral is master of all the captains."

"Like a king?" asked Jemmy.

"Yes, in a way. And the admiral of all nine ships is Sir George Somers. He is sailing on the *Sea Adventure* and we are sailing with him." Dr. Crider pointed out the window. "See the ship with the blue stripe? That's the *Sea Adventure.*"

"It's the biggest one," said Jemmy.

"The most beautiful, too," said Dr. Crider, "and she's going to be our home. Think of it. She'll be our home all the way to Virginia!"

Another day, another night, and the ships were ready. They were loaded with food and water. Everyone bound for America was on board. At sunrise on that gray morning—the morning of June 2—the *Sea Adventure* set sail. The other ships swung slowly into line behind her.

Dr. Crider stood on the main deck. Amanda, Jemmy, and Meg stood near him. People on board were weeping as they waved to people on shore.

"Why are they crying?" asked Jemmy.

"Sometimes it's sad to say good-bye," said Amanda.

"I'm glad to be going," said Jemmy. "Aren't you glad?"

She was looking out to sea at the clouds and mist that hid the sky.

He pulled at her sleeve. "Aren't you glad, Amanda?"

"Yes," she said. "I'm glad."

XI

The Hold

Jemmy liked to be on deck. "Why can't we stay up here all the time?" he asked.

"Sometimes it rains. We need a roof over us," said Amanda. "We have to live in the hold."

The hold was the long room below the deck. They lived there with more than a hundred and fifty others. When they all lay down to sleep, they were crowded together like salt fish in a barrel.

Sometimes Amanda lay awake at night. She saw men, women, and children lying all about her. In the candlelight their faces looked odd and pale. She heard them snore and moan and talk in their sleep.

In the middle of the hold was a heap of chests and boxes. Sometimes it moved a little, as if it might tumble down.

Some of the men and women on the voyage were ladies and gentlemen. They lived in rooms beyond a curtain at one end of the hold. Amanda had never seen these rooms. It was said that they had canvas walls and real beds.

Jemmy hated the hold. "The hole," he called it. When he went into it, he held his nose.

"It's just for a few weeks," Amanda told him.

"Yes," said Dr. Crider. "The voyage will be all too short."

He loved the sea. Almost every night he was gone for an hour or two. Often his hair and clothes were wet when he came down into the hold. "I like to stand by the rail and let the waves break in my face," he said.

He loved the ship. He was even happy with the food—hard biscuits, cabbages, and salt beef, salt pork, or salt fish.

"When I was a boy," he said, "I wanted to run away and be a sailor. I wish I had!"

He cared for the sick. Sometimes he was busy day and night.

"Don't you feel tired?" Amanda would ask.

"Never," he would answer.

After a week they sailed into calm waters. The days were warm.

"Now we don't have to stay in the hole," said Jemmy.

He and his sisters were on deck every day. They liked to watch the other ships.

"Will they stay together all the way?" Jemmy asked Dr. Crider.

"They will if they can," said the doctor. He knew the names of the other ships. "There's the *Blessing*," he would say. "That one is the *Catch*—and I see the *Lion* and the *Virginia* . . ."

Once he showed them three men on the deck of the *Sea Adventure*. "There they are," he said, "the captain, the governor, and the admiral. The one with the pink face is Christopher Newport. He is the captain. The thin man is Thomas Gates. He will be governor of Virginia when we land there. The man with the red beard is the admiral—Sir George Somers."

Later that day Amanda was at the rail with Jemmy and Meg when Sir George Somers came by.

"Good-day, Admiral," said Jemmy.

The man looked surprised. Then he laughed. "Good-day, young sailor," he said, and he went on up to his cabin.

"Jemmy!" said Amanda. "How did you dare speak to him?"

"He didn't mind," said Jemmy.

"But he is the admiral!"

Still she felt rather proud of Jemmy. Such a boy would grow up to be a daring man, she thought, and a daring man might have great adventures.

XII

Near the Sea

Before many days Amanda knew almost everyone on board.

There was a strong young man named John Rolfe. There was his pretty wife, who looked ill.

There were two young men who often quarreled, yet they were always together. With their long faces and thick, black eyebrows, they looked a little alike. Their names were Robert Waters and Chris Carter.

There was the Hopkins family—Master Stephen Hopkins, his wife, and their two children. Their daughter, Anne, was ten years old. Their son, David, was seven.

The Hopkins children had a ball made from a stocking. The stocking had been rolled up and tied with string. They played with it on deck. They threw it carefully back and forth and never let it fall.

Once Jemmy asked them to throw it to him.

"No," said Anne. "You might let it go into the sea."

"Come with us, Jemmy," said Amanda. "Meg and I are going to see the animals."

There were farm animals in a pen on deck. There were two goats and two oxen. There were five pigs and a flock of chickens. One of the chickens was beginning to crow. When he crowed, Jemmy crowed back.

Anne Hopkins put the ball into her pocket. She and her brother came to see the animals, too.

"We are going to have an animal farm in Virginia," she said. "There are horses on one of the other ships. Did you know that?"

"No," said Amanda.

"I rode a horse once," said Anne. "Did you ever?"

Amanda shook her head.

"Where did you live before you came on the ship?" asked Anne.

"In London," Amanda told her. "I lived in a great house."

"You must have been a servant," said Anne.

"I was," said Amanda, "but I won't be a servant in the New World."

Dr. Crider went by.

"Is he your father?" asked Anne.

"No," said Amanda.

"Your grandfather?"

"He is our friend."

Anne watched Dr. Crider as he went below. "He's strange, isn't he?"

"No, he isn't," said Amanda.

"Then why does he stand by the rail when the waves come over? Why does he let himself get wet?"

"He likes to be near the sea."

Anne gave a sniff. "The sea is all around us. Isn't that near enough?"

Toward the end of June they sailed into rough waters. One morning, after a stormy night, Amanda and Jemmy and Meg were having breakfast in the hold. John Rolfe came looking for them.

"Where is the doctor?" he asked. "My wife is ill, and we need him."

"I'll find him, sir." Amanda went above. The wind was still blowing. Only a few people were on deck.

She asked some of them if they had seen Dr. Crider. None of them had.

She went below. "He isn't on deck," she told John Rolfe.

"He isn't in the hold," said Master Rolfe.

She pointed to the rooms where the ladies and gentlemen lived. "He may be in there."

"No, he isn't," said Master Rolfe. "When did you last see him?"

"Last night."

"Not this morning?"

"No, sir."

Again she went up on deck. She even went to the galley where the cook was cutting up cabbages.

He was angry when she spoke to him.

"You can't come in here! No, I've *not* seen the doctor. How should I know where he is?"

Others were looking. They asked one another, "When did you last see him?"

A sailor came forward. "I saw him on deck last

night. I said to him, 'Doctor, there's danger. The waves are coming over, and you'd best not stay here.' But I never saw him go."

John Rolfe said to Amanda, "Go below. We'll keep looking."

She went into the hold and sat with Jemmy and Meg.

It was a long time before Master Rolfe came down. "We didn't find him."

"He must be in one of the cabins," she said. "Did you ask the admiral and the captain?"

"We've been all over the ship," said Master Rolfe. "It could be . . . Amanda, it could be that he's gone."

"Where?" she asked.

"Overboard," he said.

"Oh, no," she said. "He *couldn't* be. He's on the ship somewhere. I *know* he is. I'll find him."

But she was afraid.

XIII

The Devil Doll

Master Buck, the minister, talked to Amanda, Jemmy, and Meg.

"Dr. Crider was a good man," he said. "Now he is in a better world."

"Yes, sir," said Amanda.

But she would not believe the doctor was gone. It was like a dream, she thought, and someday she would wake from it. She would wake and find him there . . .

After a week, a sailor came to look at the chests in the hold. He found the one with Dr. Crider's medicines in it. He picked it up and set it on his shoulder.

"Where are you taking it?" asked Amanda.

"To the captain's cabin," answered the sailor.

Somehow she could not pretend after that. With the chest gone, she knew that Dr. Crider was gone, too.

He was gone, and Mother was gone, and she wanted to go away by herself and cry. But where could she go to be alone? Fear came over her. Mother had died, Dr. Crider had left them. How could she be sure that Father was waiting in the New World?

She saw Jemmy and Meg watching her, almost as if they knew what she was thinking. She tried to pretend that all was well. She sang them a song. She told them a story.

She dug into one of the chests and found some scraps of cloth.

"What are you doing?" asked Jemmy.

"I'm going to make something," she said.

"What?" he asked.

"A surprise."

By candlelight, while they were asleep, she made a doll for Meg and a ball for Jemmy. In the morning she gave them their presents.

But Meg would not take the doll. She would not even touch it.

Amanda looked at it. In the daylight, she saw how ugly it was. It had a crooked grin. The pieces of string she had used for hair looked like snakes. It was a devil doll.

The ball was not much better. It had no more shape than a bean bag.

Jemmy took it, then gave it back to her. "Could I have the door knocker?" he asked.

"It's not a plaything," said Amanda.

"I want it," he said.

It was in one of the chests. She got it for him. When they went up on deck, he showed the knocker to Anne and David Hopkins.

"A lion's head!" said Anne. She and her brother wanted to play with it.

"No, it's mine." Jemmy ran away. The Hopkins children ran after him. Now and then he stopped and knocked on the deck with the knocker. Amanda heard him say, "Knock-knock, here comes Jemmy!"

She took the ball she had made and threw it overboard. She threw the devil doll after it. Almost at once she felt better—as if she had thrown away some of her sadness, some of her fear.

XIV

Brass or Gold?

That evening they sat in the hold. Amanda was teaching Meg to sew. Jemmy was rubbing the lion's head with a piece of cloth. "The men put finger marks on it," he said.

"What men?" asked Amanda.

"Master Waters and Master Carter," answered Jemmy. "Master Hopkins, too."

John Rolfe came across the hold.

Amanda asked him, "How is Mistress Rolfe?"

"Better, thank you. Amanda," he said, "I must speak to you."

He knelt beside her. He spoke in a low voice,

"This lion's head that your brother has—what *is* it?"

"It's a door knocker."

"Where did you get it?"

"From our father."

"Then it wasn't Dr. Crider's?"

"No, sir."

"What is it made of?"

"Father said it was brass."

"Do you know what people are saying about it? They are saying it is brass on the outside and gold underneath."

She looked at the lion's head in Jemmy's hands. "How could that be?"

"They say Dr. Crider had his gold melted down and made into a door knocker."

"Why?"

"So he could take it to the New World in secret," said John Rolfe.

"But—that's foolish," she said.

"Speak low," he said. "Someone might be listening."

"It's only a brass door knocker," she replied. "It used to be on our house in London. How could people think it might be gold?"

"Someone might have told them."

"Who?"

John Rolfe looked at Jemmy.

"Oh," she said.

"And if people believe the knocker is gold," said Master Rolfe, "they can make trouble."

"It's only brass."

"But if they think it's gold, they might try to take it from you."

He left her.

She whispered to Jemmy, "Put it away."

"What?"

"The knocker. Put it away."

"Why?"

"Do as I say!"

"Crosspatch," he said. But he put the knocker into his pocket.

In the morning she took it from him. When no one was looking, she hid it in one of their sea chests.

They went up on deck.

"I want the knocker," he said.

She asked him, "Did you tell Anne and David it was gold?"

He looked down.

"Did you?"

"Yes."

"Why?"

"They thought their ball was so good. I said my lion's head was better because it was gold."

"And now people think it *is* gold. Don't you see? They'll try to take it away from you."

Robert Waters came up to them. "Could I see the door knocker?" he asked.

"I put it away," said Amanda.

"You'd better have someone take care of it for you," he said. "I'll keep it safe if you like."

"It's only brass," she said.

He looked at Jemmy, then at her. She was not sure he believed her.

XV

The Storm

The talk went on for days. Was the lion's head gold? Was it only brass? Had it been Dr. Crider's? Where had it really come from?

Then it was forgotten. There was something that mattered more. There was the storm.

It began with a few low clouds. The air was heavy and hot. It seemed to press down until everyone felt restless. Some grew angry without knowing why.

A young gentleman came out of his room and threw his dish across the hold. "The food on this ship isn't fit for pigs!" he shouted.

Mistress Hopkins talked in a loud voice, "They said we would be in Virginia in five weeks. Now it's the end of July. Seven weeks we've been at sea. How much longer will it be, I'd like to know?"

Amanda was on deck with Jemmy and Meg when the wind sprang up. It was a fierce, hot wind that burned their faces and tore at their clothes.

There was a long, blue flash of lightning, and thunder shook the ship.

They ran for the hold. Jemmy went ahead. Amanda helped Meg down the ladder.

It was dark as night in the hold. Someone lighted candles.

Amanda found a box for them to sit on, but Jemmy would not sit down.

"I'm not going to stay here," he said. "There's no air to breathe."

Robert Waters came by and gave him a pat on the head. "Don't you fret," he said. "It's just another storm. It will soon blow over."

But it was more than just another storm.

A sailor came down to look for leaks. "In all my days at sea," he said, "I've never seen such as this."

The waves were higher than the ship, he told

them. The deck was deep in water. The wind was tearing the sails to bits.

The ship rolled from side to side, and the people were thrown back and forth. Boxes and chests were thrown back and forth with them.

The hold had been closed against the storm.

"Thank heaven we're safe here," said Master Hopkins.

"You call this safe?" cried Mistress Hopkins as she dodged a sliding chest.

"At least, we're dry," said Master Hopkins.

"We won't be dry for long," she said.

The hold had begun to leak.

"To the pumps!" called John Rolfe. "All hands to help pump out the water!"

"I'll help," said Amanda.

"Not you," said John Rolfe, and she went back to Jemmy and Meg.

For two days the ship was tossed and shaken in the storm. Amanda and Jemmy and Meg clung together.

They heard Master Hopkins's voice. "The ship is sinking, the ship is sinking!"

"*Are* we sinking?" asked Jemmy.

"No," said Amanda.

"How do you know?" asked Jemmy.

"Listen to me," she said. "I—I'll tell you a story!"

"What?"

"I said I'll tell you a *story!*"

"We couldn't hear it."

"I'll *make* you hear."

Above the roar of the wind and rain, Amanda shouted, "There were two sisters and their brother. They were on a ship—and there was a storm. Can you hear?"

"Yes," he said.

"It was a great storm. It went on and on. And then—"

"What?" asked Jemmy.

"It was over, and there was—there was land."

"Where?" asked Jemmy.

"In the middle of the sea. They got off the ship—and they were safe on land."

He was quiet then. Both he and Meg were quiet for a long time.

There was another day of storm, and another night, and the ship stayed afloat. But there were new leaks. The pumps could not keep the water out of the hold.

People began to climb up the ladder and onto the deck. Amanda felt the water rising over her feet. She pushed Jemmy and Meg up the ladder ahead of her. They were on deck, and the rain and waves swept over them.

Amanda was thrown off her feet. She reached out for Jemmy and Meg. Only Jemmy was there.

"Meg!" she cried.

"She's gone!" cried Jemmy. "Meg, *Meg!*"

They tumbled across the deck and came up against the animal pen. It was broken now. The animals were gone.

"I see her!" said Jemmy.

Meg was there. She was holding on to a wooden bar of the pen.

"Don't let go!" said Amanda.

Now she and Jemmy were holding on to the pen. A woman was there beside them. She screamed each time the ship rolled.

It seemed to Amanda that hours went by. Then she felt a kind of stillness about her. She lifted her head. A little light had broken through the clouds.

A cry went up, "Land!"

There was another cry, "Rocks! We're on the rocks!"

The *Sea Adventure* rose and fell. There was a grinding, splintering crash, as if she were breaking into a thousand pieces.

XVI

Ashore

Amanda was on her feet. Something strange had happened. The deck no longer shivered and tipped beneath her. She could stand. She could walk.

She tried to look over the rail. The wind blew spray into her face.

"Get up, Meg," said Jemmy. "We've stopped."

John Rolfe and Mistress Rolfe were at the rail.

"Now I see," he was saying. "The ship is caught between two rocks."

"Then we can't sink," said his wife.

"But the ship may break apart," he said. "We must get to shore."

People were running across the deck. Sailors were making the small boats ready.

Admiral Somers shouted through a horn, "Women and children into the first boat!"

Amanda and Jemmy and Meg crowded in with the others. Men were there to row.

The boat swung down over the side. A wave lifted it high and carried it away.

Amanda was between Jemmy and Meg. They were on their knees in the bottom of the boat.

"I see land!" shouted Jemmy.

Amanda saw it, too. It was like a long shadow through the rain.

"There's land," she said, with her mouth close to Meg's ear.

Meg didn't answer. She was hiding her face under Amanda's arm.

Amanda held her breath as the boat dipped and rocked from one wave to another. They reached the shallow water near the shore. There the waves were not so high, the roar of the storm not so loud. She began to hear voices of the people about her. She heard a woman ask, "Is this Virginia?"

A sailor answered, "This is an island. The admiral says this is Bermuda."

The woman set up a wail. "Bermuda is where the devils are!"

Another woman wailed with her, "The devils made the storm and wrecked the ship. They'll never let us land!"

"Devils or not," said the sailor, "I mean to land this boat."

Amanda watched the shore. Now she could see a white strip of land next to the water, with green woods beyond.

The boat scraped the sand. The men helped the women and children out.

Amanda and Jemmy and Meg started up across the beach. It was hard for them to walk on land. They were used to the ship that kept moving under their feet.

Meg had hold of Amanda's dress. "This is your land," she said.

"*My* land?" said Amanda.

"The one you told us about."

"That was just a story," said Amanda. "I didn't know there would be land here."

"Yes, you did," said Meg.

XVII

The Island

On the island, at least, the storm was over. The small boats had brought everyone ashore. People were resting on the sand.

Admiral Somers walked among them. He spoke to them and shook their hands. "We've been through the storm and shipwreck," he said, "with not a life lost."

"What of the other ships?" asked Master Hopkins.

"I pray they are safe," said the admiral. "If they rode out the storm, they may be sailing on to Virginia."

Someone had built a fire. People sat about it, dry-ing their clothes. Most of them were ladies and gentlemen. There was no room for Amanda and Jemmy and Meg.

They found their own place. They lay down on the side of a sandbank and were soon asleep.

They slept the rest of the day and all that night. The morning sun was in their eyes when they woke.

Amanda sat up. She still felt tired, and her back ached. People were up and about. Their voices sounded far away. Beside her, Meg was saying, "There's salt in my eyes."

Jemmy was on his feet. Amanda heard him say, "The little boats went out to the wreck. See what they brought."

She saw the heap of rope and canvas and boxes and barrels on the shore.

"I think one of our chests is there," said Jemmy.

Amanda hoped so. They needed a change of clothing. The clothes they wore were stiff with salt.

A man came by. "Can you clean fish?" he asked.

"Yes," she said. She tried to get up and fell over. He set her on her feet.

She followed him to the flat rocks near the water. She felt as if she were learning to walk again.

There were fish spread out on the rocks. A man came up with another pailful.

"The harbor is full of them," he said.

He gave Amanda a knife, and she split fish and cleaned them.

Robert Waters came up with a pail in his hand. "If anyone is thirsty," he said, "I found pools of rainwater up there in the rocks. And see what else I found."

He showed them the pail nearly full of eggs.

"Almost as big as hen's eggs," he said. "They are from the white birds you see along the shore."

"We'll live like kings here," said an old sailor, "if the devils don't get us first."

"There are wild pigs in the woods," said Robert Waters, "and they have no fear of me. It's like they never saw a man before."

"You saw no devils?" asked the old sailor.

Robert Waters shook his head.

"Since I was a boy, I've heard of the Bermuda devils," said the sailor. "Now I think there are no devils here and never were. Sailors from Spain found these islands long ago. They wanted Bermuda for themselves, so they told tales to keep everyone else away."

Master Waters took the knife from Amanda. "I'll clean fish for a while. Go and have some food."

A kettle was boiling over the fire. The ship's cook stood by with a long spoon in his hand.

Amanda and Jemmy and Meg waited in line. Each one was given a wide, thick leaf from a palm tree. Onto each leaf the cook spooned a piece of fish and two eggs.

They went to the edge of the woods, out of the hot sunlight. Amanda helped Jemmy and Meg take the fish off the bones.

"This is good," said Jemmy. "Isn't it good, Amanda? Is there more?"

"We'll see," she said.

Meg rolled up her leaf and made a nest for her two eggs. "They're pretty," she said.

"Poor little Meggie," said Amanda. "Your dress is all shrunk. It's up to your knees."

"So is yours," said Meg. "You look funny."

"We all look funny," said Jemmy, but no one laughed. They couldn't laugh yet, thought Amanda. They felt beaten and tired. The sound of the storm was still in their ears.

XVIII

The Smallest House

Now that they were on land, Sir Thomas Gates was their governor. He set them to work.

They moved away from the harbor where the sun beat down on the sand. They built a village among the trees. Some of the houses were tents. Others were made of rocks, logs, and branches.

The children helped cut the long leaves from palmetto trees and spread them in the sun. When the leaves were dry they were used to make roofs.

Governor Gates told Amanda and Jemmy and Meg, "You are to live with the Hopkins family."

Mistress Hopkins said to Amanda, "I have my

87

own children to look after. Why must I look after three more?"

"You needn't look after us," said Amanda.

"I must," said Mistress Hopkins, "as long as the governor says we are to share our house with you."

Amanda went to the governor. "If it please you," she said, "my brother and sister and I want to live by ourselves."

"You must live with someone else," he said, "until we can build more houses."

"We can build our own," she said.

"Can you, indeed?"

"Yes, sir," she said.

"Try if you like," he told her. "You'll find it not so easy."

They cut branches and carried rocks. They began to build their house at the edge of the village, under a cedar tree.

They put up a wall of sticks, rocks, and mud. When it fell over, people laughed.

But others came to help. Before many days the house was done. It was the smallest one in the village, but there was room for them to sleep, and there was a place for their sea chest. They were

proud of their house. Amanda made a broom of palmetto leaves, and she swept the dirt floor every day.

Jemmy said, "We're going to stay here, aren't we?"

"No. We're going to Virginia," said Amanda.

"Some of the men say we're going to stay in Bermuda. They say no one else lives here, and we can have all the land we want and plenty to eat—"

"We're *not* going to stay here," said Amanda. "The sailors are putting a deck on one of the small boats, and it will sail to Virginia."

"How many will *that* hold?" said Jemmy.

"We'll not all be going," Amanda told him. "Only a few will go. Then they'll send a ship back for us."

They went down to the bay where men were at work on the small boat. Master Ravens was there. He was a tall man with great arms and a thick neck. He was to be captain of the boat.

Amanda asked him, "How long will it take you to sail to Virginia?"

"A week," he said. "Maybe two."

"When you see our father, will you tell him we

are safe in Bermuda—Jemmy and Meg and I?"

"That I will," he said.

"His name is James Freebold."

"I know," said Master Ravens. "I'll not forget."

The boat sailed late in August. Amanda was there with the others to wave good-bye. The boat looked so small in the great ocean. It looked so very small.

XIX

A Fire at Night

On a summer evening Amanda and Jemmy and Meg sat outside their doorway. Amanda was sewing a shirt for Jemmy. Meg was making a hat of green palmetto leaves. Jemmy was rubbing the door knocker with a cloth.

Robert Waters and Chris Carter came by. Barefooted, with their long black beards, they looked like wild men. They stopped for a look at the lion's head.

"It was in our chest," said Jemmy, "and the salt water made spots on it."

"Shall I take them off for you?" asked Master Carter.

"I can do it," said Jemmy.

The two men went away, but in a little while Master Waters came back alone. "Do you like palmetto berries?"

"Yes," said Jemmy.

"Do you know the place where the men dug the new well? I saw berries on a tree a little farther on."

After Master Waters had gone, Jemmy said, "I'm going to get some berries."

"We'll all go," said Amanda.

They walked through the woods. Meg was skipping.

Amanda asked her, "Where did you learn to skip?"

"I don't know," said Meg. "It just happened to me."

They went as far as the new well and a little farther. They found no palmetto berries, but they found something they had never seen before. It was a big, smooth rock with moss on its sides.

Jemmy climbed up on it and jumped off.

"I want to jump," said Meg.

She climbed the rock. She jumped off and fell into the bushes.

Amanda went to her. "Did you hurt yourself?"

"No," said Meg. She began to pull at her buttons.

"Meg!" said Amanda. "What are you doing?"

"I can't jump in all these clothes." Meg was out of her dress. She kicked off her shoes. Barefooted and in her petticoat, she climbed the rock and stood there.

"Look at me!" she shouted. "I'm a bird!"

She jumped, with her long hair flying.

Amanda looked in wonder. Meg was playing. Here on this island, in the clear, bright air, she had learned to play!

Jemmy was shouting, "I'm a bird, too!" He climbed the rock and jumped after her. Again and again they jumped.

"Come and jump, Amanda," said Jemmy.

"Oh, no," she said. It was such a long time since she had played. She was sure she had forgotten how.

They walked slowly home. The sun was nearly down when they came to their house.

Jemmy looked into the sea chest. "Where is the knocker?"

"Where did you put it?" asked Amanda.

"Back in the chest."

"Are you sure?"

"I *thought* I put it back," he said.

He looked in the grass outside the house. Anne Hopkins came down the path.

"What are you looking for?" she asked.

"My lion's head," he said.

"Maybe someone took it."

"Who?" he asked.

Anne didn't answer.

"Maybe *you* took it," he said.

She pulled her lips in. "Do you think I would ever steal or tell a lie? *I* mean to go to heaven!"

September passed, and part of October.

Every night a fire was lighted on the north tip of the island. It was to guide the ship that would come from Virginia.

But when November came, Admiral Somers said, "We need not light the fire any longer. I fear the boat never reached Virginia. If it had, a ship would have come by now."

XX

A Quarrel

Winter on the island was like no winter Amanda had ever known before. The days were fair. Warm winds blew in from the sea.

In the north harbor men were building a ship. Part of it was made of wood from the wrecked *Sea Adventure*. Part of it was made of cedar that had been cut on the island.

Almost every evening Amanda and Jemmy and Meg took a walk down to the north harbor to see the ship that was being built.

"It looks like a fish with the bones picked clean," said Jemmy.

There was a long, wooden keel with wooden ribs fastened to it. It *did* look like the bones of a fish, thought Amanda.

Before the ship was finished, Admiral Somers said, "We must build another one."

"Why?" asked the men.

"This ship will not hold all our people and the things we want to take," said the admiral. "And there is another reason. If one ship should be lost, the other might still reach Virginia."

Some of the men were angry. "We have worked hard," they said, "and now more work is put on our shoulders."

A cloud seemed to fall over the island. Men began to meet in small groups. They talked together, and their voices were low and secret.

A quarrel broke out on the north harbor.

Amanda and Jemmy and Meg met Mistress Hopkins outside her house. Mistress Hopkins talked to them about what had happened.

Some of the men said they were tired of building ships. Why should they go to Virginia, they said, when they had a good life here?

"We must go to Virginia," said Admiral Somers.

"The people there need our help, and we were sent to help them."

"Go if you will," said Robert Waters. "Some of us mean to stay."

He and seven others stopped work. They went to live on the other side of the island.

"It doesn't surprise me," said Mistress Hopkins. "Robert Waters was always one to make trouble."

Anne Hopkins was in the doorway.

"Is Master Waters gone?" she asked.

"Yes," said his mother.

"And he isn't coming back?"

"So he says," said Mistress Hopkins.

"Then I can tell," said Anne. "I was afraid of him before, but now I can tell."

"Tell what?" asked her mother.

"He took the lion's head."

"How do you know?" asked Amanda.

"I saw him go into your house while you were gone," said Anne, "and you never saw the lion's head after that."

"Master Waters was good to us," said Amanda. "He helped build our house. I don't believe he would take the door knocker."

"You don't have to believe me," said Anne, "but I know what I saw."

Amanda and Jemmy and Meg went home.

"Do you think Master Waters took the door knocker?" asked Amanda.

"He used to say someone might steal it," said Jemmy. "He used to say he wanted to keep it for me."

"Do you think he has it now?" asked Amanda.

"I don't know," said Jemmy.

XXI

Waiting for Jemmy

One by one the men came back, until only Chris Carter and Robert Waters were left.

Work went on at the north harbor. Both ships were finished.

"We may reach Virginia in a week," said the admiral, "but it could be longer. We must carry enough food and water to last six weeks."

Men began loading the ships with fresh water, pickled eggs, salt fish, and salt pork. Word was given to everyone in the village, "Be ready to sail on the tenth day of May."

"What of Master Waters and Master Carter?" someone asked.

"They chose to stay," said Admiral Somers, "so let them stay."

Two days before the tenth of May, Amanda and Meg got up in the morning to find Jemmy gone.

They were only a little anxious. Sometimes he went to the beach to see the sunrise. Sometimes men took him fishing.

But by evening he had not come home.

Amanda went to Governor Gates. "My brother is gone," she said.

"The boy who likes to roam about the island?" said the governor. "Go home. He may be there now."

But Jemmy did not come home that night.

The next morning Amanda and Meg set out looking for him. They looked along the beach and in the woods.

"This island is too big," said Meg. "There are too many places."

Back in the village, they went from house to house. "Have you seen Jemmy?" asked Amanda. "Will you help us find him?"

People were packing their boxes and sea chests and helping load the ships. Only a few left their work to look for Jemmy, and they stopped looking when evening came.

"But Jemmy is *lost!*" cried Amanda.

"How can we look in the dark?" said one of the men, and Amanda and Meg were soon left alone.

They went back to their house.

Meg asked, "Will the ships sail tomorrow?"

"I think so," said Amanda.

"Even if Jemmy isn't here?"

"He will be here," said Amanda. "Go to bed."

"Aren't you coming?"

"Not yet," said Amanda.

"I want to stay up with you."

They sat in the doorway. Amanda tried to see out into the night.

"What if Jemmy doesn't come back?" asked Meg.

"Then we'll stay here till we find him."

"But the ships are going tomorrow."

"They will go without us."

"Will they let us stay?"

"If they don't, we can hide," said Amanda. "We can hide till the ships are gone."

"How will we ever get to Virginia?" asked Meg.

"We'll think about that later," said Amanda. "We can't leave Jemmy, can we?"

"No," said Meg. "Amanda, do you hear a sound that's like talking?"

"It's the wind. It makes that sound in the cedar tree." Amanda stood up. "Oh, Meggie, it's so dark out there! If Jemmy did come back, how could he find us?"

She went into the house and felt on top of the sea chest for their one candle. She found it. "Wait here," she said.

Their cook fire was out. She went up the path until she saw a few coals still burning in someone else's cook fire. She knelt by the coals and lighted the candle.

She went back to Meg. She stood in front of the house and held the candle high.

Almost at once she heard footsteps. The candle shook in her hand. She almost dropped it.

"Jemmy?"

It *was* Jemmy. She could see him against the darkness.

"Amanda, I got it," he said.

"What?" she asked.

"The knock-knock," he said.

XXII

The Other Side of the Island

It was the tenth of May. The two ships had sailed. From the deck of the larger ship, Amanda and Jemmy and Meg looked back at the island.

"It's nearly gone," said Amanda.

"It looks so little," said Meg.

"It looks little from here," said Jemmy, "but it's a big island. You'd know, if you'd been lost there."

"Tell about being lost," said Meg.

"I told it already."

"You told Amanda. I went to sleep. Now tell me."

So he told his story again. He had gone into the

woods to find Robert Waters. "I knew there wasn't much time before we sailed," he said. "If Master Waters did have my lion's head, I wanted it back."

But he had lost his way. When night came, he had to sleep in the woods.

"In the morning I called and called, and they found me—Master Waters and Master Carter. They took me to their camp. I said I wanted the lion's head. Master Waters said he was keeping it so nobody would take it from me. He said we might get back to England one day, and then we could sell it for money."

"Did you tell him it wasn't gold?" asked Amanda.

"Yes, but he didn't believe me. Master Carter told him to give it back. Master Waters wouldn't, and they started to fight. While they were fighting, I went into the tent and found the knocker. I took it and ran."

Once he had thought Master Waters was after him.

"I hid under a bush," he said. "I hid till after dark; then I came on. I didn't know where I was till I saw the candle out in front of our house."

"Why didn't you tell us where you were going?" asked Amanda.

"I didn't know it would take so long," he said.

"You made us all worry, Jemmy." Yet she was proud of him. Whatever he did, it seemed she was proud of him.

The two ships were crowded. They were more crowded than the *Sea Adventure* had been. But the sea was calm, and the voyage was easy. In less than two weeks, they were in sight of land.

The ships sailed side by side into the waters of a bay.

Captain Newport had sailed these waters before. "Chesapeake Bay," he said.

Amanda saw a rooftop on shore. A flag was flying from it.

"Is it Jamestown?" she asked.

"No," said the captain. "That is the fort on Point Comfort."

They stopped at Point Comfort. Two other ships were there.

Captain Newport and Admiral Somers began to point and talk together in great excitement. The ships they saw were two that had sailed with the *Sea Adventure!*

A man rowed out from shore in a canoe. Sailors

threw him a rope and pulled him aboard.

He was a gray-haired Englishman. "Have you come from England?" he asked.

"From Bermuda," answered the admiral. "I am Admiral Somers, and our ship the *Sea Adventure* was wrecked there."

The man cried out. "This is a great miracle! We thought you were lost!"

"What of the other ships that sailed with us?" asked the admiral.

"All but one came safely to Virginia."

"Where are they now?"

"Gone back to England, except for those you see here, and they will leave soon."

"What of Jamestown?" asked Captain Newport.

The Englishman shook his head. "Ah, there's a sad tale."

Amanda was listening. She drew near.

"There was war between the English and the Indians," the man said. "Our people were ill and starving. It was a terrible winter. Once five hundred of us lived in Jamestown. Now only a handful are left. Some went away into the woods. Some are dead. We hear that more ships are on the way from England. I pray they will come in time to save our poor colony."

"*We* are here," said Admiral Somers. "Let us go to Jamestown with all speed."

XXIII

The Lion's Head

The ships sailed up a river with woods on either side. It was the River James, said Captain Newport.

Amanda and Jemmy and Meg were on deck. Jemmy was watching for Indians. Meg was watching for deer.

"What are you watching for, Amanda?" she asked.

Amanda hardly heard. She was saying over and over to herself, Let Father be safe, let him be well . . .

They came in sight of Jamestown.

"It's on an island," said Master Rolfe.

"*Almost* an island," said the captain.

The town was inside a wall made of tall tree trunks. A few gray rooftops rose above the wall.

Captain Newport shouted through a horn, "Hal-loo!"

Only an echo came back.

A party of men landed just down the river from Jamestown. Amanda watched them make their way along the shore.

"What are they doing?" she asked a sailor.

"They are making sure it is safe for us to land," he answered.

Soon the men were in the town, looking out over the wall. They were making signs to let the captain know there was no danger.

"The river is deep here," said the captain. "We can bring the ships all the way to shore."

The ships came up almost under the wall. Admiral Somers and Captain Newport crossed the plank from their ship to the shore. Ladies and gentlemen began to cross after them.

Amanda and Jemmy and Meg waited their turn. Someone made way for them, and they walked across the plank.

On shore, they followed the others to a gate in

the wall. It was open, and they went through. They saw a square of log houses, a church, and a long shed that might have been a storehouse. The roof was off the shed. The church door was broken.

There was an open yard in the middle of the town. A few thin, wild-looking men were there. They had gathered about the admiral and the captain.

Amanda looked quickly at their faces and turned away. She looked into houses, one after another. All were empty.

Halfway around the square she went, looking, looking—

She pushed open the door of a house and drew back. A man was there.

He lay on the floor. His clothes were in rags, and he was so thin the bones of his face stood out.

He was changed. He was so terribly changed, yet she knew him.

"Father," she said.

He turned toward her. His eyes were staring, and he said something that sounded like, "They've gone away!"

"Father, it's Amanda," she said.

Still his eyes stared. He didn't know her. She

wanted to cry out, Look at me! Remember me!

Jemmy and Meg were in the doorway. They came slowly inside.

"Is it Father?" whispered Meg.

"Is it, Amanda?" asked Jemmy.

"Yes, but he doesn't—he doesn't—" She knelt and tried again. "It's Amanda and Jemmy and Meg."

Jemmy came closer. He had taken the lion's head out of his pocket. He was holding it up for Father to see.

And Father saw it! He was *looking*—first at the lion's head, then at their faces. He spoke their names. "Amanda. Jemmy. Meg."

Amanda dried her eyes on her sleeve. She said to Jemmy and Meg, "Go to the admiral, go to the captain. Ask them to come here, and then you go to the ship. Bring food—anything you can find. Bring water."

They started off.

"Run!" she said.

She took Father's head in her lap. He reached up a hand to her, and she held it. She had thought it might be cold, but it was warm.

She was not afraid now. They were here to care

for him—she and Jemmy and Meg—and help was on the way.

He was looking toward the door. She looked to see what he had seen. Above the door latch was a peg, and Jemmy had hung the knocker there. The lion's head had caught the light and made a brightness in the room.

Historical Note

On June 2, 1609, the *Sea Adventure,* with eight other ships, sailed from Plymouth, England. The small fleet was bound for Virginia, then an English colony in the New World. Two years before, settlers had founded the village of Jamestown there. Now many were ill, they faced starvation, and they were at war with the natives.

The ships from England were bringing help and supplies. For weeks they sailed together, but on July 23 a storm drove them apart. Three days later the *Sea Adventure* was wrecked off an island in the Bermudas, about six hundred miles from Virginia.

There were men, women, and children on board. All landed safely. In the nine months they lived there, they built two ships, and in May, 1610, they sailed to Virginia. They brought food from the friendly island—salt fish and pork, palm cabbage, cactus pears, and the pickled eggs of wild birds.

They found Jamestown almost deserted. After the winter of 1609–10, known as the Starving Time, only a few settlers were left. The colonists from Bermuda fed and cared for them. Before the food was gone, three ships came from England with more supplies and new settlers, and Jamestown was saved.

Stories of the *Sea Adventure* were published in England. Some of them were read by a man who wrote plays for the London theater, and he wrote a play about a storm at sea and a shipwreck on an enchanted island. The play was *The Tempest*. The man was William Shakespeare.

About the Author

CLYDE ROBERT BULLA is one of America's best-known writers for young people. The broad scope of his interests has led him to write more than fifty distinguished books on a variety of subjects, including travel, history, science, and music. He has received a number of awards for his contributions to the field of children's books, including, for *Shoeshine Girl,* awards in three states—Oklahoma, Arkansas, and South Carolina—the winners of which were voted upon by school children.

Clyde Bulla's early years were spent on a farm near King City, Missouri. He now lives and works in the bustling city of Los Angeles. When he is not busy writing a book, he loves to travel.

About the Artist

A recent graduate of the Rhode Island School of Design, Michele Chessare is a comparative newcomer to the field of children's book illustration. Her drawings have appeared regularly in the *New York Times Book Review* and in a number of other magazines, including *Saturday Review, Rolling Stone,* and *Rocky Mountain* magazine. Ms. Chessare lives in Upper Montclair, New Jersey.